After their great adventure discovering the Land of Milk and Honey, Henry and Sam and Mr Fielding decide to settle down in life.

Alas! Sam's children are so noisy that he can't work on his Memoirs. Henry's wife is so house-proud that it's driving him around the bend. And Mr Fielding's offspring are eating all before them, so that he hardly gets a bite to eat.

Suddenly they get a letter. Uncle Bert Bigger has been kidnapped! So the three mice become Special Agents to join in the rescue.

The journey takes them, by plane and sleigh, to the North Pole, where they meet an old friend, Stamper, and make two new ones — Will the Wizardene, and Pat the snowman (from Connemara).

Can they track down the terrible STAR (spell it backwards) gang and their leader Evil, and rescue Uncle Bert and Roberta?

And can they stop STAR from destroying Sam's home — Wicklow parish church.

GW00729032

Vera Pettigrew

Henry & Sam & Mr Fielding
Special Agents

Illustrated by
Terry Myler

THE CHILDREN'S PRESS

To
my family and friends

First published 1992 by
The Children's Press
45 Palmerston Road, Dublin 6
Reprinted 1993

© Text Vera Pettigrew
© Illustrations The Children's Press

ISBN 0 947962 72 7 paper

Origination by Computertype Limited
Printed by Colour Books Limited

Contents

WICKLOW

1
The Letter

Sam the church-mouse sat in his study writing his memoirs. Long ago when he was young, he had had a wonderful adventure with Henry the house-mouse and Mr Fielding the field-mouse. They travelled far and wide to the Land of Milk and Honey and even beyond. They met many strange creatures and found Mr Fielding's long-lost Uncle Bert Bigger. The journey was often dangerous and sometimes the mice thought they would never see home again. But at last, flying on the backs of the wild geese, they did get home.

The years passed and now Sam had a wife and many children. He could hear his children now, talking, laughing, arguing, with loud music playing, for all day long in his house there was noise.

Sam sat staring at an empty sheet of white paper and not another word could he write, for Sam had run out of memories.

Postie-mouse walked up the path to the church door. Half way there he stopped and stared at the letter he carried. He turned it this way and that and even held it up to the sunlight.

'What cheek,' thought Sam as he hurried out to meet him, and taking the letter he went inside and closed the door.

'For the Special Attention of Sam the church-mouse,'

he read, and turning the envelope over he saw, in large letters, the word URGENT.

'Strange,' he thought, 'who can be writing to me in such a way?' Tearing the letter open this is what he read. ·

Dear Sam,
My husband Bert Bigger has been kidnapped. Please come at once with Mr Fielding and Henry.
                                    Signed Bertha Bigger.

'How terrible,' said Sam to himself as he remembered the happy times spent at the Bigger House. 'I must tell my friends,' and out of the church he ran.

Mr Fielding lived in a warm, cosy stable. He and his family had plenty to eat, which was lucky for they all loved food. Once his wife had opened a restaurant. Mice came from all over County Wicklow to eat there, but as Mr Fielding ate more than the customers, it had to close.

Mr Fielding sat by the stove remembering the days of the great adventure and he grew sad thinking of the times that were past.

'Perhaps I'll have something to eat,' he thought, 'that will surely cheer me up,' and he heaved his fat body from the chair and waddled across the kitchen. He opened the fridge and eyed the delicious pie left there for supper, but as Sam arrived at that moment, and Mr Fielding was so pleased to see him, he forgot all about food.

'Come in,' he called. 'I'll make a pot of tea,' and he quickly put the kettle on.

'My friend,' said Sam, 'I come with bad news,' and he read Aunt Bertha's letter.

'How dreadful,' wailed Mr Fielding. 'Poor Uncle Bert. We must go at once, this very minute — I'll just pack some food.'

'We must go first to Henry's house,' replied Sam, 'and plan our journey.'

'What I'd like to know,' said Mr Fielding as they set out, 'is why did Aunt Bertha write to you and not to me? After all I'm her nephew?'

'You know the answer to that,' replied Sam. 'You have never learned to read.'

Henry the house-mouse stood at his sitting-room window looking out. His house was called the Big House and he lived in style. He too had a wife and many children but there wasn't a sign or a sound of a mouse child anywhere for they were all watching TV.

In his house were many rooms all furnished with every comfort, but as his wife Henrietta was very house-proud, she cleaned and polished, brushed and scrubbed all day long. He could hear her now making everything spick and span. Henrietta hated noise, except for cleaning noise, so when the children watched TV, which was all day long, they wore headphones so that the sound wouldn't disturb their mother. The TV room was very large and there wasn't just one set, there were dozens, so that each child could watch his or her favourite programme.

In her spare time Henrietta was writing a book. *Handy Hints for House-Mice* it was called and it was going to be a best-seller. At the top of every page in large letters was written BEWARE OF CATS. Henry thought that the best Hint of all, for he and his family had had some unpleasant encounters with cats.

Outside his house was a garden full of flowers, but Henry didn't go out much because of the TERROR, and worse still because of the TERROR'S daughter. At first she was a playful little kitten and no harm to anyone but as time went by she grew bigger and fiercer. The TERRIBLE TERROR the mice called her, or TT for short.

Henry stood looking at the sunshine and the green grass and he longed to go outside. He thought of happy days travelling with his friends through fields and woods, and the more he thought the sadder he felt, and two big tears fell 'plop' on his stylish red slippers.

Suddenly he saw a movement outside and, to his great joy, crossing the lawn were Sam and Mr Fielding. Running to the front door he threw it open and drew them inside.

'Is something wrong?' he asked when he saw their unhappy faces.

'Bad news,' said Mr Fielding.

'The worst,' said Sam and he read Aunt Bertha's letter.

Henry's shoulders began to shake and loud sobs echoed through the room.

'Poor kind Uncle Bert,' he sobbed and his crying grew so loud it nearly drowned Henrietta's house cleaning.

'What are *you* crying for?' asked Mr Fielding. 'He's *my* uncle, not yours.'

'I was fond of him,' sniffed Henry, dabbing his eyes on a large yellow hankie.

'All this boo-hooing won't get us anywhere,' said Sam severely. 'We must sit down calmly and quietly and plan our journey.'

The hours passed and the mice grew weary and upset, for try as they would they could not remember the way to the Bigger House. Eventually they gave up and decided to meet again on the morrow.

As Henry showed his friends to the front door Mr Fielding turned and looked at him. 'Are you ill?' he asked.

'Not in the least,' answered Henry. 'Why do you ask?'

'I see you are wearing your dressing-gown and slippers,' said Mr. Fielding.

'I always wear them,' replied Henry. 'There's no point in getting dressed as I never go outside.'

'That fellow gets odder and odder,' said Mr Fielding as he and Sam walked quickly through the garden, keeping an eye out for cats. 'And he didn't even offer us a cup of tea.'

As the mice drew near their homes Sam thought of the noise that awaited him and he shuddered. Mr Fielding thought of the delicious pie for supper and he grew anxious, wondering if his children would have eaten every scrap.

'You know,' he said, 'I think another adventure might be the very thing for us.'

'I couldn't agree more,' replied Sam as the two friends parted.

2
A Special Assignment

Sam stood outside the church in the quiet darkness as the clock struck midnight. He couldn't sleep, for his mind buzzed with the problem of how to find the Bigger House. Long ago when he travelled with his friends they had a map. But the map had been lost, never to be found.

With a sigh he turned and went indoors. For once all was quiet as his children slept. His wife Samantha was asleep too. When Sam had shown her Aunt Bertha's letter she became very angry.

'You are too old,' she said, 'to go on a wild-mouse chase,' and off she went to bed in great annoyance.

Sam was so exhausted by all this upset that he slept late. He didn't waken until Samantha brought him a morning cup of tea.

'Well,' she said frostily, 'I don't approve of this journey to find Bert Bigger, but if you must go, I suppose you must.'

'We won't be going anywhere,' answered Sam, 'if we can't remember the way,' and he lay back against the pillows and closed his eyes.

Presently he heard an unusual noise outside, coming closer and closer.

'That sounds like a plane,' he thought, 'and a low-flying one at that.' Out of bed he jumped and ran to the window and sure enough, just skimming the tree-tops, was a small silver plane.

'Gracious me,' he thought, 'I hope it's not going to crash,' and flinging on his clothes he ran outside, followed by his whole family.

Henry too slept badly. When he told his wife of Uncle Bert's kidnapping and that he and his friends had a special assignment to find him, Henrietta began to sob wildly.

'You can't go,' she cried. 'Your place is here with me and the children. Who will mend the TVs and the cleaning equipment when you are gone?'

It had all been most distressing, but at last he dropped off to sleep, to dream of the Land of Milk and Honey.

He was getting up when he heard a plane flying low over the garden. Downstairs Henrietta was starting her cleaning and the children were tuning their TVs when all of a sudden they began experiencing interference.

'Father,' they shrieked, 'there's something wrong with our TVs.'

'I do believe that plane is going to land,' Henry thought in alarm, and forgetting all about Handy Hint No 1 — BEWARE OF CATS — he ran outside.

Mr Fielding had slept very well indeed. When he had said good-bye to Sam and arrived home there was great excitement in his house for his children were going to a disco. There was noise and bustle everywhere as they got ready, but when Mr Fielding looked in the fridge for the lovely pie for supper, it was gone.

He called angrily to his wife but she too was in a hurry, for it was the evening of her ICA meeting, which of course means Irish Countrymice Association! When at last she heard what Mr Fielding was saying, she called out, 'The children must have eaten it but there's another one in the freezer. You can have the whole thing.'

When his wife had gone and all his children had disappeared, Mr Fielding put the pie into the microwave to defrost. When it had thawed, he popped it into the oven and it came out crisp and delicious and he ate every scrap. Then he made a pot of tea and as he sat by the warm stove he thought about Uncle Bert.

'I hope he wasn't eaten by wild animals,' he thought, and as he began to feel quite frightened by his imaginings, and quite full in his stomach, he went to bed. As he dropped off to sleep he remembered that he hadn't told his wife about Uncle Bert.

'I'll tell her in the morning,' he said to himself, and before you could wink, he was snoring loudly.

Mr Fielding was eating breakfast when he heard a plane. In fact it was his second breakfast. The first was eaten with his wife as he told her about the kidnapping.

'Well one thing is sure,' she said. 'You are so fat and unfit you couldn't rescue a fly.'

Then Mr Fielding became very angry and his wife became even more angry and some fiery words passed between them. Afterwards Mr Fielding felt so weak he had to make a pot of tea and fry some sausages.

As he finished the last mouthful he heard the plane. Lumbering to the door he saw to his amazement a little silver plane coming in to land on the field beside his house. As it taxied to a halt every mouse in the countryside appeared, running and scampering, squeaking with excitement. Sam and his family came streaming out of the woods, and even Henry arrived,

followed by Henrietta and all their children.

'What do you make of this?' he panted. 'Is it some kind of invasion?'

'We will soon know,' answered Mr Fielding, as the door of the plane opened and the pilot appeared.

'Well I must say,' said Sam, 'whoever he is, he's a jolly good pilot.'

'You're getting short-sighted, my dear,' said his wife. 'Can't you see it's not a he at all. It's a *she*!'

And so it was.

3
Kidnapped

As the pilot crossed the field the young mice crowded round her asking excited questions. There was such a throng she couldn't take even one step. But at last the crowd parted and she made her way towards Henry and Sam and Mr Fielding.

'Do you not remember me?' she asked. 'I'm Roberta, Bert Bigger's daughter.'

When the mice recovered from that shock, they went inside Mr Fielding's house and shut the door against the crowd, and Roberta, who had been a tiny mouse-child when they last saw her, told them the sad tale of Uncle Bert's kidnapping.

'My father is rich,' she said, 'and travels the world on business. It was on his last trip, piloting his own plane, that he disappeared.'

'But who could have kidnapped him?' asked Sam in alarm.

As Roberta handed him a sheet of paper he turned pale. 'Oh no,' he said. 'Not *that*.'

'Tell us,' cried Henry and Mr Fielding in agitation. 'Don't keep us in suspense.'

'STAR,' said Sam and his voice was only a whisper.

'STAR,' gasped Mr Fielding and he began to shiver and shake.

'I don't understand,' cried Henry. 'I'm only a house-mouse and not wise in worldly ways.'

'The Secret Service,' whispered Sam.

'The Underground Movement,' croaked Mr Fielding.

'*What* Secret Service? *What* Underground Movement?' shrieked Henry.

'Spell STAR backwards,' said Roberta. 'Then you will know.'

So slowly and carefully Henry spelt out the letters ... R-A-T-S ... and with a loud cry he fainted.

When Henry felt a little better and Mr Fielding made a pot of tea, Sam said, 'Not a word of this to our wives. If they learn who has kidnapped Uncle Bert we will never be able to leave.'

And so the mice prepared for the journey,

In the Big House Henry was packing.

'You'll need warm clothes,' said his wife. 'Strong shoes, extra socks and a travelling iron,' and she bustled about, getting everything ready.

In Mr Fielding's house his wife was baking.

'Good nourishing food,' she said. 'That is what you'll need and plenty of it,' and Mr Fielding quite agreed.

At Sam's house he and his wife sat in the study and Sam wasn't packing at all. After a while he put a few small things into a rucksack.

'What about your mouth-organ, dear?' asked Samantha.

'Too noisy,' replied Sam. 'If I played that, the whole world would know we were coming,' and fastening the straps of his rucksack he went to bed.

'Don't forget your glasses,' called Samantha but Sam was already asleep.

In the small hours before dawn Roberta Bigger was checking her plane. As the moon grew pale and the stars faded, Sam and his family arrived. Next came Mr Fielding and his family carrying a large hamper of food.

'Why do you want that?' asked Roberta. 'It's not necessary you know.'

'Yes it is,' answered Mrs Fielding. 'I want my husband well fed on this trip.'

Out of the woods hurried a strange figure in a long dark cloak and a black hat, his eyes hidden by sunglasses.

'Who is that?' asked Roberta as the figure drew near.

'Bless my whiskers,' said Sam. 'It's Henry!'

'Why are you dressed like that?' asked Mr Fielding. 'It's most odd.'

'Ah ha,' said Henry, as he removed his dark glasses, 'You didn't recognise me, did you? It's my disguise. Henrietta made it.'

'Who are you disguised from?' asked Sam.

'The enemy, of course,' replied Henry.

At those words Henry's children wept loudly and wailed at the tops of their voices.

'This crying won't do,' said Sam. 'It will upset all our families,' and indeed it had, for every mouse-child began to bawl and the three wives dabbed their eyes with tissues.

'All aboard,' called Roberta as a last farewell was said.

'My trunk,' gasped Henry. 'You're forgetting my trunk,' and there standing beside the plane was a large trunk with the initials H H M painted on the side.

'What's that for?' asked Sam.

'My belongings,' answered Henry. 'Henrietta packed it for me,' and in went the trunk with not an inch to spare.

The plane taxied to the end of the field as the mice, with much waving, took to the air.

4
The Adventure Begins

The silver plane circled while down below the mice could see their families still waving. They saw Mr Fielding's home and Sam's Church and the Big House, and then banking steeply they set course.

Over the river, the fields and the woods they flew, the mice pointing excitedly at all they saw, but after a time they grew silent, thinking of their wives and children, wondering when they would see them again.

'Let's have something to eat,' said Mr Fielding. 'That would do us good.' But when he unbuckled his seat belt and moved cautiously to his hamper, he found Henry's trunk wedged tightly on top.

Mr Fielding was most annoyed.

'I can't understand,' he said, 'why you need all those clothes. It's quite ridiculous.'

'I can't understand,' replied Henry, 'why you need all that food. It's really disgusting.'

Well, what an argument developed. Sam wondered what Roberta must be thinking until he saw her shoulders shaking with mirth.

'You're making a laughing-stock of yourselves,' he said sternly to his friends. 'Stop it at once.'

Suddenly the plane began to shudder and shake.

'What's happening,' cried the mice in alarm as they clutched their seats.

'It's an air-pocket,' replied Roberta calmly. 'It will be over soon.'

'Are you an experienced pilot?' asked Sam when his heart stopped beating overtime.

'Very,' replied Roberta. 'I've been flying for years.'

'Who taught you?' inquired Mr Fielding.

'My father did,' answered Roberta. 'He taught the whole family, even my mother.'

As they flew quietly on, Henry sat thinking of all the Biggers buzzing along in their planes.

'They must cause a lot of TV interference,' he thought. 'The noise would drive Henrietta distracted,' and he felt glad he didn't live near them.

Without warning the plane began to shiver and shake again. The mice sat tense and not a little afraid.

'We didn't have this air turbulence,' whispered Sam, 'when we flew with the wild geese.'

'We certainly didn't,' said Mr Fielding. 'Our flight was as smooth as silk.'

'And warm too,' said Henry as he remembered nestling between the wings of the geese.

'Are you cold?' asked Roberta, who had heard every word they said, and she turned on the heating.

'Poor old things,' she thought. 'They are very out of date. I hope my mother was right to send for them.'

On they flew and as the mice grew warm and relaxed, they fell asleep.

When they awoke the plane was making its descent. The sun was sinking in the west like a ball of fire, turning the sky crimson. Now they saw the woods where the Biggers lived, as lower and lower they flew until it seemed they would touch the very tree-tops. But the trees thinned, a runway appeared and they landed without a bump or a jolt.

'Well done,' called the mice as Roberta brought the plane to a gentle stop.

'I must say,' said Sam, 'you're a jolly good pilot.'

Roberta opened the door and the mice climbed stiffly down. They breathed the cool evening air and were glad to have arrived.

Just then Roberta's brothers and sisters came running.

'How is your mother?' Sam asked as they walked through the woods.

'Greatly distressed,' replied her son Albert. 'This kidnapping is terrible.'

At the Bigger house Aunt Bertha was waiting. As she kissed the mice her tears flowed warm and wet over them. When she grew calm they all sat down to tea and what a feast they had! Then they talked and talked until the mice grew weary and their eyes closed with sleep.

'Time for bed,' said Albert at last. 'Tomorrow we will plan the rescue.'

So once more Henry and Sam and Mr Fielding slept in the Bigger bedrooms that were furnished with every luxury, and no sooner had their heads touched the pillows than they fell asleep, snoring loudly.

When they awoke it was morning, and it was raining.

Sam looked out of his bedroom window and his spirits were as grey as the sky. He opened his rucksack and rummaged inside.

'I haven't even a mac,' he thought. 'I'll get a dreadful cold.'

Then to his delight he saw his mouth-organ. Samantha had packed it after all. As he put it to his lips and began to play, his spirits lifted.

Mr Fielding heard Sam playing and as he hated the mouth-organ it put him in a bad temper. He opened his bedroom door and sniffed the air, but there wasn't even a whiff of breakfast.

Henry peered into his trunk deciding what to wear. 'Perhaps my velvet jacket,' he thought, 'or my leather waistcoat,' but in the end he chose a pullover made by Henrietta. When he saw the rain pouring down he put on his yellow mac and red boots too.

After a while the sound of voices could be heard

as the Bigger children came jogging through the woods. As they streamed into the house chattering loudly, Sam thought, 'They're just as noisy as my own children.'

Henry thought, 'That racket would drive Henrietta wild.'

And Mr Fielding thought, 'Perhaps now we'll get some breakfast.' And indeed they did and it was everything a mouse could desire.

When the food was eaten and the tea drunk, the mice and all the Biggers held a meeting.

After many hours talk and much discussion, it was decided to fly four missions to the furthest corners of

the globe to search for Uncle Bert.

'I'm a little surprised,' Sam said to his friends when the planning was over, 'not to be leading one of the missions myself.'

'Why you?' asked Mr Fielding. 'Why not Henry or me?'

'Have you forgotten,' replied Sam, 'that I led you most successfully on our last expedition?'

'I remember we got lost,' answered Mr Fielding. 'If it hadn't been for the wild geese we would never have seen home again.'

Then Sam's blood boiled with anger and turning his back on Mr Fielding he ignored him for the rest of the day.

As Henry packed a small rucksack, he looked sadly at his trunkful of clothes.

As Mr Fielding packed, he thought with longing of his hamper full of food.

As Sam packed, a tremor of excitement ran through him, for in his rucksack was a map.

'Guard it carefully,' said Albert.

As the sun rose over the tree-tops on a bright clear morning, the rescue operation prepared to leave. As the mice boarded their plane, the South-bound mission was leaving, flying to the heat of the desert.

'I'm glad we're not going there,' said Henry. 'I'd hate all that sand.'

'What do you know of the desert?' asked Mr Fielding, 'I thought you never left your house.'

'I saw it on TV,' replied Henry. 'A most unpleasant place.'

As the East mission took to the air, Sam said, 'I've always fancied a trip to the Orient. A most exotic place!'

As Roberta taxied to the end of the runway, the West-bound plane left.

'Well, that's one place I wouldn't want to go,' said Mr Fielding. 'All those cowboys and bucking broncos.'

Last of all the mission to the North took to the air, with Henry and Sam and Mr Fielding on board. As Roberta set course, they saw the lonely figure of Aunt Bertha on the runway below.

5

The Mission to the North

As the plane set course Sam opened the map and, spreading it on his knees, he began to read.

'Land of Cats,' he said with horror. 'Do we really fly over that?'

'We do indeed,' replied Roberta. 'It's most interesting.'

'What if we crash?' asked Mr Fielding weakly.

'We won't crash,' answered Roberta. 'Just relax and enjoy the flight.'

The time passed and the flight was smooth and comfortable. They crossed the sea where white-capped waves tossed wildly, but the mice grew more anxious by the minute for the Land of Cats was approaching fast.

'Have you a camera?' Roberta asked. 'If we fly low enough you could get some good photos.'

'No, thank you,' said Sam hastily. 'We won't bother with photos today,' but already Roberta was skimming the tree-tops.

The mice looked down with horror at what they saw below. There were cats walking and running, sitting and creeping. Cats of every age, size and colour.

'What a nightmare,' thought the mice and they closed their eyes, feeling faint and weak.

On they flew and as the light faded they could hear

yowling and fighting and see cats' eyes glowing in the darkness.

But the Land of Cats passed and the mice breathed a sigh of relief.

'We will land soon,' said Roberta. 'It's time to sleep.'

'That will be in No Man's Land,' said Sam, consulting the map. 'What horror will we find there?'

'No horror at all,' answered Roberta. 'It's quite safe, neither man nor beast live there; it's only a resting place.'

Down glided the plane, lower and lower, until they touched the ground. The night was dark with no stars. The mice looked out fearfully, but Roberta jumped down without a moment's hesitation.

'Come out,' she called. 'The air will do you good.' But it was three nervous mice who followed her.

When they had eased their aching limbs and breathed deeply of the night air, they all stretched out in their plane seats and fell asleep at once.

When they awoke, Roberta was outside, jogging.

'You should try it,' she called. 'It's really good for you,' but the mice were too busy eating breakfast to hear her.

On they flew and No Man's Land stretched as far as the eye could see, a great expanse of grey where nothing moved.

When darkness fell they landed again.

'The Land of Clouds,' said Sam, reading his map.

'Yes,' replied Roberta, 'and tomorrow it will rain.'

Again the mice slept. When they awoke the rain poured down and Roberta had disappeared.

The three mice peered anxiously out on a landscape hidden in mist and not a foot from the plane could they see.

'Perhaps she's jogged further than usual,' said Henry.

'That's it,' agreed Sam. 'She'll be back any second.'

But the seconds turned to minutes and the minutes to an hour, and still Roberta did not come.

'Maybe we should call,' suggested Mr Fielding, but although they called and called, no answering voice was heard.

'We must search for her,' said Sam. 'She may be ill or have fallen down a hole.'

As the mice stepped outside with fast-beating hearts, the rain had eased but the mist swirled round them. Before they took even one step, they saw hanging on the side of the plane a sheet of paper.

'What is this?' asked Sam, peering closely.

With a cry of terror he fell back. As Henry and Mr Fielding looked at that paper their blood ran cold, for there was the dreaded sign.

'STAR,' they whispered as they sank to the ground in horror.

When the strength had returned to their legs, the mice fled back into the plane and banged the door shut.

'They are out there now,' moaned Henry. 'Watching us.'

As the mice looked through the windows at the blanket of mist, they were sure they could see the great gleaming eyes and yellow–fanged teeth of the rats as they dragged Roberta away.

'We've forgotten the radio,' shouted Sam. 'We'll

contact Aunt Bertha and someone will save us.'

But when they tried it, the radio was dead.

'We are lost,' cried Henry. 'We will never see our families again,' and he began to sob.

'One thing is sure,' said Sam. 'We can't go back; we would never survive the Land of Cats. We must press on. Be brave, my friends, we will crush the enemy yet.'

At those stirring words the mice grew calm.

'Well,' said Sam, 'it looks as if I'll have to lead the expedition after all.'

'And why you?' asked Mr Fielding. 'What about me?'

Well, how those mice argued.

'We'll take a vote,' Sam said at last. 'All those in favour of Sam the church-mouse as leader stand up,' and he jumped quickly to his feet, followed by Henry.

'Traitor,' hissed Mr Fielding and he gave Henry a *terrible* look.

'That settles it,' said Sam. 'I win by a majority of one.'

'Oh no you don't,' said Mr Fielding angrily. 'We haven't counted my votes yet. All those in favour of Mr Fielding as leader stand up,' and up he leaped, followed by Henry.

'This is ridiculous,' said Sam, looking sternly at Henry. 'You can't vote for both of us.'

'You ask me to choose between my two friends,' said Henry in great distress. 'That I'll *never* do.'

Then the mice grew silent until Sam spoke. 'You, Henry, are a true and loyal friend,' he said. 'I am ashamed of myself.'

'I am too,' said Mr Fielding, and all was forgiven and forgotten.

And so the mice prepared to leave the plane.

'It's a pity,' Sam said to Mr Fielding, 'that you never learned to fly a plane like your cousins. They are all very competent mice.'

'And where would I have learned?' replied Mr Fielding snappily. '*You* can't even ride a bike.'

'Oh don't fight again,' cried Henry. 'We'll get nowhere if you do.'

'You're right,' said Sam. 'All our nerves are on edge.'

And so with wildly thumping hearts the mice left the plane.

'Keep close together,' whispered Sam.

'Don't make a sound,' breathed Mr Fielding, as off into the cold dampness they crept. When they looked back, the plane had disappeared into the swirling mist.

Their last link with civilization was gone.

6

The Land of Clouds

Through the mist stumbled the mice, their bodies almost touching. In spite of their thermal underwear they shivered.

'Keep close to the trees,' advised Sam.

'Don't step on rustling leaves,' warned Mr Fielding.

'Are we being followed?' asked Henry over and over again, but the only sound was the 'drip, drip' of the trees.

Sam checked his compass often to be sure they were travelling north, as on they went through the mist, looking and listening with all their senses alert.

As they stopped for a rest a worm slithered by.

'Excuse me,' Sam said in a low voice. 'Have you seen any rats lately?' The worm said nothing but slid on faster than ever.

Round the corner a snail appeared.

'You there,' said Mr Fielding. 'Did you meet any rats today?' but the snail just disappeared into his shell and there he stayed.

On the mice went, but whenever they met a slug or a beetle and asked the same question, they all hurried off without a word.

'What a shady lot,' said Mr Fielding.

'And unfriendly too' said Henry.

'There's something here I don't like,' replied Sam,

'I fear we may be in danger,' but as evening approached nothing happened.

When the mice were so tired they couldn't take another step, and so hungry they had grown weak, they struck camp and pitched their tent deep in the undergrowth. After a supper of bread and cheese, they climbed into their sleeping-bags and fell fast asleep.

Some time in the small dark hours of the night they awoke. Shivers ran up and down their spines for they heard the sound of many feet, coming nearer and nearer: 'Tramp, tramp, tramp,' as if a whole army were on the move. The mice cowered in terror as the feet passed only inches from their tent.

The marching died away, the night grew silent, but it was nearly dawn before they slept again.

When they awoke the mist had gone and the morning was cool and fresh.

'We must hurry,' said Sam. 'If that was STAR who passed in the night they must be far ahead.'

They hadn't walked more than a dozen steps when they heard again the sound of tramping feet.

Along the path came an extraordinary sight. With dozens of feet marching in time, came a family of centipedes; mother, father and two children.

When the mice saw them, they burst out laughing, for their terror had turned to joy.

'What's so funny?' asked the mother. 'We have a problem that's no joke. Our children have worn out all their shoes and we have no money to buy new ones.'

'We have to keep them walking,' said the father, 'or their feet will drop off with the cold.'

'How terrible,' said Mr Fielding as he looked in horror at the children's chapped, cold feet.

'I wish we could help,' said Sam, 'but we carry no money.'

'I can help,' said Henry, and taking needles, thread and scissors from his rucksack, he cut the pockets clean off his yellow mac. And what do you think he did then? He snipped and sewed, sewed and snipped, and in no time at all forty pairs of little yellow boots lay on the grass, all ready to wear.

How excited the centipede children were as they put them on and stamped around proudly.

'Who taught you to do that?' asked Sam in amazement.

'Henrietta did,' answered Henry. 'I make all my family's shoes.'

As the children ran up and down the path playing, the mice told the parents their story.

'We haven't seen rats for a long time,' the centipides said, 'but you never know, they could be just around the corner.'

And so they parted, and the little yellow boots went 'thump, thump, thump, thump' and the sound of their marching could be heard for many a mile.

A flock of birds flew overhead, wheeling and calling, but the mice didn't notice them. They didn't even notice an old animal hobbling slowly along in front, until they nearly bumped into him.

'I beg your pardon,' said Sam when he saw the creature was wearing dark glasses and carrying a white stick. 'Can I help you, for I see you are blind?'

'Yes indeed,' whined the tall gaunt figure in a long tattered coat. 'It's a hard life for some.'

So Sam took his arm and guided him carefully along.

'It's good to help the old and feeble,' he thought, but Mr Fielding was thinking something else.

As the old creature limped along he left large footprints behind, and the footprints were those of a rat!

'We've been tricked,' screamed Mr Fielding.

With a snarl the rat turned and flinging off his disguise he leaped at Mr Fielding. Catching him by the throat he began to shake him with all his might.

But help was at hand. Round the corner came the centipedes. As two hundred pairs of feet kicked and thumped the rat, he dropped Mr Fielding. With a scream he took to his heels but before he disappeared from sight he turned, and with ferocious rage called out, 'I am leader of STAR. My name is Evil. You will suffer for this.'

Mr Fielding lay on the ground gasping for breath. 'That was a near one,' he said shakily.

40

Then the centipedes told how the birds had seen Evil and how they flew over the countryside calling a warning. 'We thought you were in danger,' they said, 'so we followed you. We were never far behind.'

As the day was now much advanced and the rain had begun to pour down once more, the mice stopped for the night. As they put up their tent, father centipede said, 'We will stay close by tonight and will come if you need us.'

In the morning a watery sun appeared. Sam checked the map and set his compass.

'We will soon reach the Valley of Peace,' he said.

On they went fearfully, expecting the enemy every moment but there was no sign of him, and no sign of Roberta either.

Many hours later, weary and footsore, the mice passed a herd of deer grazing in the damp pasture.

'Are we near the Valley of Peace?' asked Sam.

'Just ahead,' answered the deer. 'You can't miss it.'

As the mice approached the border, a figure in a dark uniform and cap stepped out from the trees.

'Passport Control,' he said. 'Have you anything to

declare — any guns or ammunition?'

'What is this?' asked the mice in alarm. 'We know nothing of guns or ammunition.'

'Perhaps you have a map,' said the figure. 'Hand it over.'

At that moment Sam saw under the cap, the gleaming rat eyes of Evil.

'Run,' he shouted and, not a moment too soon, the mice ran, right in amongst the herd of deer.

As Evil tried to follow, the deer closed ranks.

'Stand back,' they roared. 'Be off with you or we'll stamp you into the ground.'

With a blood-curdling cry Evil bolted, but as he did he screamed, 'I will get you yet.'

'We will take you across the border,' the deer said, 'In the Valley of Peace you will be safe.'

'Surely we will meet Evil and STAR there,' answered the mice and they told the deer of the kidnapping.

'In the Valley of Peace no rats are allowed,' said the deer. 'They must travel the long way round.'

And so the mice crossed the border safely and as Sam set his compass for the north they wondered what lay ahead.

7

The Valley of Peace

The sun shone as the mice walked in a beautiful green valley. The soft buzzing of insects filled the air and butterflies flitted from flower to flower. Above, in a clear blue sky, larks sang at the tops of their voices. The mice felt relaxed and happy with thoughts of STAR far away, for they knew they were safe in that place.

Henry took off his yellow mac and packed it in his rucksack. Mr Fielding and Sam rolled up their sleeves as the sun shone warm on their bodies.

Suddenly they heard a sneeze coming from behind a gorse bush.

'Who is it?' whispered Henry and the mice stood quietly listening.

'A-tish-oo,' went the sneeze again.

'There's one way to find out,' said Sam, and round the bush he strode.

Sitting in a little pram all by herself was a baby hedgehog.

'Hello,' said Sam. 'Where is your mama?'

But the baby just bounced up and down in delight.

'She's too young to talk,' said Henry and he began to play a game of 'peep'.

Down the path came mother hedgehog. When she saw the mice with her baby she was very angry.

'You woke her,' she stormed. 'How dare you.'

'Madam,' said Sam coldly, 'you had no business leaving her alone. She might have been kidnapped.'

'What nonsense,' said the mother. 'There is no kidnapping in the Valley of Peace,' and off she hurried, pushing the little pram.

'Boo-hoo-hoo,' bawled the baby and her cries grew louder and louder.

'It seems she likes you,' said the mother in surprise.

At that moment the rest of the hedgehog family arrived. 'Join us for a picnic,' they said as they spread a red check tablecloth on the ground.

So the mice sat down on the warm grass and what a time they had.

As they were about to leave Sam asked, 'What do you know of STAR?'

'Never heard of it,' replied father hedgehog.

'Do you know any rats?' asked Mr Fielding.

'No, thank goodness,' said the mother. 'Those creatures were banished from here years ago.'

On the mice went and the Valley stretched broad and wide in the sunshine.

They came to a wood and there gathering nuts was a red squirrel.

'Where are you going?' he called when he saw the mice. But when he heard their story he grew thoughtful. 'Are you not a little too old,' he said, 'for that kind of adventure?'

'Not in the least,' replied Sam, nettled.

'We're as fit as fiddles,' said Mr Fielding.

'What cheek!' muttered Henry. 'That fellow has no respect,' and they pulled in their stomachs and walked with a swinging step to show how young they were. But when the squirrel was out of sight, they stopped walking for they felt in need of a rest.

As they rested, through the tall grass came a strange looking mouse. He had a light brown coat with a dark stripe and a very long tail.

'Hi, there,' he called. 'Who are you guys?'

When the three mice had introduced themselves, the newcomer said, 'I'm a Northern Birch mouse myself.'

Then Birch invited them to his home and it was a very nice home indeed, with a grass roof and walls of soft moss.

'Stay a while,' he said. 'I'd be glad of the company.'

So the mice stayed and they all talked and talked. When they grew tired, Birch hung three little hammocks from the ceiling and Henry and Sam and Mr Fielding climbed into them and they were as cosy as can be.

'I'm off now,' said Birch. 'I sleep by day and go out at night,' and away he went before the mice could say a word.

In the morning, as they got up, the sun was shining and Birch was coming in through the front door.

'Time for breakfast,' he said taking down the frying-pan. So the mice had breakfast and it was quite a feast.

'You must stay a little longer,' said Birch as they washed the dishes. 'Tonight I will show you the golden horses who guard the Valley of Peace.'

So the day passed and they all rested in the drowsy heat.

As the sun set Birch awoke. 'We must hurry,' he said, 'for it will soon be dark.'

Through the Valley they went and in the last rays of the sun they saw the horses grazing in the lush green pasture. Their coats shone like gold and their manes like silver, and never had the mice seen any animals so beautiful.

'Welcome to our Valley,' said the stallion as he raised his great head and looked at them. 'Travel safely and go in peace.'

As the moon rose the mice said good-bye to Birch.

'If you stayed another day,' he said, 'I could show you my winter house. It's right underground and very comfortable.'

'We *have* to leave,' said Sam. 'We *must* carry on with our mission. We must find Uncle Bert ... and Roberta.'

As the mice travelled the night creatures rustled in

46

the undergrowth and a bat or two swooped past. After a time they camped beside a little stream and with the sound of running water in their ears they fell asleep.

And so the mice journeyed on. Through meadows scented with flowers, through woods dappled with sunlight. They saw the golden horses often as they patrolled the Valley, and they thought how good it must be to live in that place.

Now, as they drew near the border, they could see the Magic Mountain rising hazy blue in the distance.

On the tree-covered slopes of the Magic Mountain a great grey owl was flying. She was tired for she had flown a long way. When she crossed the border to the Valley of Peace she was nearly home. Far below in the moonlight she saw the three mice. The owl was hungry and her eyes grew round with longing for a nice mouse stew, but she knew she would be banished for ever from the Valley if she touched them.

'Those fellows are going somewhere,' she said to

herself when she saw they carried rucksacks. 'I wonder what's up?' and being a curious bird, she had to find out.

Down she swooped, but when the mice saw her they ran with cries of terror into the undergrowth.

'I won't harm you,' called the owl softly, but it was some time before the mice came creeping out.

When they recovered from the fright they told their story.

'You are brave little animals,' said the owl. 'I wouldn't be in your shoes for anything.'

'Have you seen STAR lately?' asked Sam.

'I saw them two days ago,' replied the owl. 'Heading north.'

'Had they prisoners with them?' asked the mice.

'That I can't say,' answered the owl. 'It was snowing hard at the time.'

As the mice prepared to travel on they shivered in the cold night air.

'You need warmer clothing,' said the owl. 'I have a bag of feathers to spare. Take them with you; they might come in useful.'

So the owl flew home, the mice slept, and when the sun rose they left the Valley of Peace and crossed the border to the Magic Mountain.

8

The Magic Mountain

When the mice crossed the border to the Magic Mountain the air grew chill with a hint of snow.

Sam took the map from his pocket and spread it on the ground. He set his compass and when the needle steadied it pointed north up the mountainside.

'This will be a hard climb,' he said. 'Our strength will be taxed to the full.'

The mice looked at the path ahead winding steeply between dark trees and they all felt great fear.

'We'll never make it,' wailed Henry. 'We are too old for this kind of thing.'

'We can't give up now,' said Mr Fielding. 'Think of Uncle Bert and Roberta,' and shouldering his rucksack he strode bravely ahead.

'Have courage, my friend,' said Sam as he and Henry followed. 'We will succeed yet.'

The forest was dark and silent with no sunlight, as up the path they struggled. Their feet made no sound for a carpet of pine needles covered the ground. The air grew colder still and the mice began to shiver.

'That great grey owl gave us some feathers,' said Sam, 'but what will we do with them?'

'I know!' said Henry, and taking needles and thread from his rucksack, he set to work.

Sam and Mr Fielding watched in amazement, as

before their very eyes, three waistcoats, three cosy hats and three scarves appeared.

'Well I never,' said Mr Fielding. 'Who taught you to do that?'

'Henrietta did,' answered Henry. 'I make all my family's clothes.'

So the mice put on their waistcoats, hats and scarves, and they were as warm as toast.

On they walked and the snow began to float lightly down.

As darkness fell the forest grew spooky. The mice pitched their tent and crawled inside. They opened their rucksacks and out spilled a load of goodies that Birch had given them. They ate and ate until they couldn't eat any more. As they snuggled into their sleeping-bags, outside in the dark forest the snow fell softly.

In the morning Mr Fielding opened the tent flap and looked out. He turned pale and sank back with a moan.

'What is it?' asked Sam in alarm.

'Is it Evil?' whispered Henry in fear.

'It's a huge animal,' gasped Mr Fielding. 'As big as a house, quite terrifying.'

When Sam had summoned up his courage, he peeped out. There was indeed a huge animal outside, with great branching horns on his enormous head.

'It's an elk,' he said. 'The tallest animal in the northern forest.'

The elk pulled twigs and leaves from the snow-covered bushes, munching noisily. After a while he stopped eating, his nose twitching as he smelt the air.

'Who's there?' he called, and walking towards the tent his large feet made deep prints in the snow.

The mice clung together, expecting any moment to be squashed flat. When the elk was only a few feet away he stopped.

'Well, well,' he said. 'It's three little mice. No wonder I couldn't see you,' and he roared with laughter.

And what a nice elk he was, as he joked and chatted. 'I hope we'll meet again,' he called when the mice waved good-bye.

A raven flew over the trees with a loud cry, while up amongst the branches a nutcracker bird pecked at a pine cone. The sound of running water filled the air as a slow-flowing river came in sight.

'What's that?' asked Henry pointing to a large pile of sticks rising from the water.

'It's a lodge,' replied Sam. 'The home of a beaver.'

At that moment two beavers appeared, swimming

up river with branches in their mouths. They carefully added these to their home.

'Those lads do much damage,' said Sam. 'They fell whole trees to build their houses.'

As the mice talked one of the beavers left his house building and swam towards them. As he climbed out of the river his thick brown coat glistened with water. He was very angry.

'If there's one thing I dislike,' he said, 'it's advice from strangers.'

'We didn't mean it that way,' replied Sam.

'We certainly didn't,' said Mr Fielding.

'Well that's how it sounded to me,' answered the beaver. 'I know your type, finding fault with everyone. If you want to criticise think what humans do.'

'You're right,' said Sam. 'They're a destructive lot.'

'They set traps for mice,' said Henry. 'They treat us very badly.'

'You look quite prosperous to me,' answered the beaver. 'Who are you anyway?'

When he heard their story the beaver called his wife.

'Ma,' he shouted, 'come and listen to this.'

'I have seen those rats,' she said. 'They crossed the river three days ago.'

'How did they cross?' asked Sam.

'By raft,' she replied. 'And a hard time they had. They were nearly swept away.'

'Had they prisoners with them?' asked Mr Fielding.

'That I don't know,' she answered. 'But here come the children; perhaps they can tell you.'

Up the river swam six noisy youngsters, shouting

happily together but when they were questioned, not one had seen a prisoner.

'We must press on,' said Sam, but when he looked at the broad river his courage failed him.

'Is there no other way to cross?' he asked.

'None,' said Pa. 'But never fear, we will help you.'

And so the beavers built a raft and with the mice on board they towed it safely to the other side.

As the mice shouldered their rucksacks and pulled on their feathered hats, the beaver children began to snigger and giggle.

'Watch your manners,' warned Ma, 'or you'll be off to bed before you know it.'

'Let me tell you,' said Pa, 'you won't see mice like these again. It's not often one meets Special Agents.'

As the mice left the river they looked back, and there working away again, building their house, was the whole beaver family.

Darkness fell and the night grew bitter with bright stars. The mice put up their tent and huddled shivering inside. No sleep came that night for the grip of winter was all around.

9

The Wizardene

In the morning the snow fell thick and fast. As the mice set off their feet sank deep.

'We'll freeze to death,' puffed Mr Fielding.

'We'll die from exhaustion,' panted Henry.

Even Sam said, 'I must admit we're ill-prepared for this.'

But they struggled on, slipping and floundering. As dusk crept into the forest icy fingers clutched at the mice. When they could take not one step more they came to a clearing amongst the trees and there, standing all by itself, was a log cabin.

As the mice crept close to the open door they saw firelight flickering on the walls inside and the smell of cooking wafted on the night air.

As they stood weak and exhausted, a voice called out.

'Come in, my friends. I've waited for you all day.'

'It's Evil,' moaned Henry. 'I know his voice,' and the three mice sank down in misery in the snow.

But it wasn't Evil! Out from the cabin came a strange figure. Covering his long skinny body were a pair of tatty jeans and a purple tee-shirt. On his curly red hair was a bowler-hat.

'Come in,' he said, 'I've long expected you.'

When the mice could move their frozen limbs, they

stumbled out of the cold and into the warmth. Drawn up by the stove, where logs crackled and burned, was a table set with food.

As the mice removed their sodden clothing and warmed their shivering bodies, the strange figure placed steaming dishes before them.

'Eat,' he said.

The mice ate the hot nour-  ishing food and they grew warm and comfortable. Not a word was spoken until every scrap was finished.

At last Sam spoke.

'My dear Sir,' he said, 'how did you know we were coming?'

'The forest animals told me,' said their host, 'that three small, half-dead mice were crawling up the mountainside.'

'May we ask who you are?' said Mr Fielding. 'You've saved our lives.'

'I'm Will,' he replied, 'the Wizardene.'

'You mean spells?' asked the mice in alarm. And gathering up their belongings they ran for the door.

'Come back,' called Will. 'I'm your friend and want to help you.'

But it was three anxious mice who came slowly back.

'You should sleep now,' said Will. 'You're quite worn out.'

So the mice stretched their aching limbs before the stove, and all was peace and quietness, while outside in the dark forest the snow lay deep.

When they awoke it was morning. A shaft of sunlight shone in through the open door, but of Will there was no sign.

On the stove a pot of coffee bubbled and on the table rolls and butter stood ready.

'Help yourselves,' said a note propped against the sugar. And that is just what they did.

When all the food was eaten and all the coffee drunk, they went to the door and looked out.

The trees stood tall in the frosty morning, their branches heavy with snow. On the cabin roof icicles hung like diamonds, while smoke from the chimney drifted upwards towards a bright blue sky. Willow-tits and brambling flew twittering here and there. A mountain hare, as white as the snow itself, hopped past, leaving footprints with his large furry feet.

'How beautiful,' said the mice as they gazed at the scene before them.

In the still cold air, someone was cutting logs and the sound echoed through the forest.

'I wonder who that is?' said Sam.

'Perhaps it's Will,' replied Mr Fielding. And sure enough, when the chopping stopped, through the forest he came.

'Good-morning,' he called. 'How are you today?'

'Fit and well,' answered the mice as they stepped out to meet him.

Will put logs on the stove, placed chairs in front of it and said, 'Little mice, you have a tale to tell. Let's have it.'

And so the day passed with much talk, as they explained about Uncle Bert Bigger and Roberta and the kidnapping.

As evening drew near, Sam looked at the books in Will's house, and as he saw the titles he grew uneasy again.

Deadly Magic, he read, *Spellbound*, and many more.

'Are you good at magic?' he asked in a shaky voice. 'Can you do all those spells?'

'Indeed and I can't,' replied Will sadly. 'That's the problem. To pass my exams and become a fully qualified wizard, I must remember them all.'

'Exams are awful,' said Henry, shuddering. 'Quite dreadful.'

'What do you know of exams?' asked Mr Fielding. 'I never heard of *you* doing any.'

'My children do them,' replied Henry. 'All the time.'

'My daughter, Miss Fidelma Fielding, won a scholarship,' said Mr Fielding smugly.

'My son Harry won a scholarship too,' answered Henry.

'Miss Fidelma gained 100% in her exam,' said Mr Fielding. 'Could your son beat that?'

'Stop all this one-up-mouseship,' ordered Sam (whose children hadn't won anything at all). 'This boasting is quite disgusting.'

As the mice prepared once more to sleep, safe and warm by the stove, Will said, 'Tomorrow we'll have a party. That's one spell I *can* do.'

In the morning there was much activity as Will prepared for his party.

'I'm really good at this spell,' he said as he gathered his ingredients.

When all was ready, he placed a large black pot on the table, and putting everything in, he began to stir with a wooden spoon.

> *Spell, spell, lightly burn,*
> *Make my wish at every turn,*

he chanted.

At first nothing happened. Then he stirred faster and faster, saying the words louder and louder. Suddenly there was a bang and the room filled with thick yellow smoke.

The mice ran in fear behind the cupboard, but when the smoke cleared, the room, to their delight, was indeed ready for a party.

Balloons hung from the ceiling, there were crackers on the chairs and presents on the floor. The table simply groaned with food. There was even a cake with lighted candles, just like a birthday.

'Well done,' called the mice. 'You're a clever lad.'

They ate the food, pulled the crackers, opened the presents and Will blew out the candles and cut the cake.

Then they played games like hide-and-seek and blind-man's-bluff. They made so much noise and laughed so loudly that the forest animals came creeping up to see what was going on.

'Come in,' called Will. 'Join the party.' Soon the cabin was filled with hopping, running creatures.

'Let's dance,' said Sam and out came his mouth-organ and he played a happy tune.

'How I hate that mouth-organ,' moaned Mr Fielding, but presently even he joined in the dance.

When everyone was tired out, the forest folk left with much calling and laughing, for never had there been such a party.

As the mice and Will stood outside saying good-bye, through the trees a white figure came skiing. As he sped along, the ends of his red scarf streamed behind him and his large black hat fluttered in the breeze.

'Who is it?' asked the mice.

'It's Pat,' said Will in delight. 'He's a real good guy,' as into the clearing skied a large snowman.

10
The Snowman

As the snowman removed his skis, Will said, 'Meet my new friends. They're Irish, like you.'

'Is that a fact?' replied Pat, as he propped his skis against the cabin wall. 'From what part do you come?'

'From Wicklow,' answered Sam. 'The Garden of Ireland.'

'I'm from the West meself,' said Pat, 'from Connemara.'

'There's not much snow in Connemara,' said Sam.

'There's surely not,' replied Pat. 'That's why I'm here. If ye'll stay quiet a while I'll tell you a bit of a yarn.

'Some years ago,' he began, 'a fall of snow covered the Twelve Ben Mountains in the County Galway. Up the mountainside comes a wee boy and girl with their Dada and they build a mighty fine snowman. There that snowman stood surveying all before him and there was no better view in the whole of Ireland. Then along come some right eejits and they slide the snowman down the mountainside to Maam Cross, where there was no snow at all. Well the snowman was in a right fix but, having a brain in his head, he jumps in the lake nearby and there he stays, nice and cool. A Garda car comes flying by and out leap the two grandest Guards in Connemara.

' "What are ye doing in the lake?" says they.

' "You may well ask," replies the snowman, and he tells his tale.

' "Well," says those two grand men, "we can't have this snowman melting away on us altogether. We'll be the laughing-stock of the West."

'So they send for a freezer truck and in goes the snowman. They whisk him away to Galway where a plane stands ready. Then they pack him in his ice-box and they fly him to this very land of the Far North.

'Now who do you think that fine snowman was?' asked Pat as he finished his story.

'I think it was you,' answered Henry.

'Good man yourself,' said Pat. 'You're right so. That snowman was me.'

'Do you miss Ireland?' asked Mr Fielding. 'Surely you get homesick.'

'Not a bit of it,' replied Pat. 'I've the great lot of friends here.'

'You've missed a party,' said Will. 'You should have come earlier.'

'I would if I'd known,' replied Pat. 'You're the hard man not to invite me.'

'Come inside,' said Will. 'We'll have some more fun now.'

In they went and the games began again until they were all puffed out.

'Let me get me breath back,' gasped Pat and down he sat beside the stove.

As they rested, a puddle began to form on the floor. To their amazement the mice saw that Pat was melting.

'Snakes alive!' shouted Pat. 'Let me out of here!' and dashing to the door he wrenched it open and ran outside.

'I'll do a spell,' cried Will and he grabbed a book from the shelf.

'Forget about spells,' shrieked Pat. ''Tis water I want and quick.'

So the mice and Will ran about with buckets and jugs of water. Some Pat drank and some they threw over him, and in the cold air he froze hard again.

'That was the fright of me life,' he said. 'I must be getting soft in the head to sit by the stove.'

Suddenly a great howling rent the air and echoed through the dark forest, as a pack of large grey wolves ran panting into the clearing. The mice took to their heels into the cabin and slammed the door tight shut.

As they peeped out of the window an extraordinary

sight met their eyes in the cold moonlight! Crouching in a circle were twelve wolves and sitting with them were Will and Pat.

As they watched Will called, 'Come out, little mice, the wolves have something to tell you.'

Out crept the mice fearfully and as they huddled together, the pack leader spoke and at last they learned something of Uncle Bert and Roberta.

'On the night of the last full moon,' he said, 'we saw the most wicked of all rats, called Evil, and his followers travelling towards the frozen north. With them they had a prisoner, a female mouse.

'Many full moons past,' continued the wolf, 'we saw a small plane circling lower and lower before landing on the ice. Out from the nearby forest came the band of rats called STAR. They dragged the pilot, an elderly mouse, from the plane and binding his legs and feet they threw him on a sleigh and set off at a run. That was the last we saw of them and all we have to tell you.'

'You have told us much,' replied Sam. 'We are truly grateful.'

When the wolves left Pat put on his skis. 'The devil take those rats,' he said. 'But never fear, we'll beat them yet.' With a wave of his hand he skied off through the forest.

The mice slept once more by the stove but their dreams were troubled by large grey wolves with great shining eyes.

In the morning the snow was falling from a dark leaden sky. Will brought a sleigh to the door calling,

'Get a move on there, we're going to visit Pat.'

'Hop on,' he said when the mice appeared. When they were settled, with a warm rug tucked round them, Will set off pulling the sleigh behind him. As it slid over the frozen ground it rocked a little from side to side, but the mice held on tight.

After a while they heard singing and along came Pat, speeding on his skis.

'That's the grand day,' he called, as the snow fell thick and fast.

He led the way along tracks piled so high with snow that it took Will all his strength to pull the sleigh. Ahead were snow-covered rocks with a narrow entrance between them, and through it he glided.

'Welcome to me home,' he said, and what a strange home it was! The floor was dark rock and from the walls hung many icicles. The ceiling was so high it was impossible to see where it ended. Pat's home was an ice-cold cave.

'Did you ever see the likes of this?' he asked with a grin on his happy white face. 'Isn't it the grandest house?'

'Very nice,' said the mice as their teeth chattered, for never in their whole lives had they been in so cold a place.

'Sit yourselves down,' said Pat cheerfully. 'Take a bite to eat,' and he placed before them a plate of iced buns.

'No, thank you,' said Sam. 'We've just had breakfast.'

'I'll have a few meself,' said Pat and he began to munch and crunch.

'What do you do in the summer?' asked Mr Fielding. 'Is it too hot for you?'

'That's a bit of a problem,' replied the snowman, 'but when I can't go out I stay in bed,' and he pointed to a large stone tub filled with ice standing in the corner. 'You may not think it,' he said, 'but that's the finest bed in the whole world.'

When at last they went outside again the mice had grown so cold their bodies were numb.

As they stood shivering and shaking, Pat asked, 'Can you lads ski?'

'A little,' answered the mice, 'but that was many years ago.'

'Well, if you're going to go north to rescue your friends, you'll need to ski,' and in a flash he had them fitted out with skis.

'Follow us,' he called as he and Will set off.

The mice dug their poles into the snow and slid their skis along. Slowly and carefully at first they went. Then faster and faster until they were nearly flying.

As evening drew near the skiing party stopped at last.

'Come home for a chat,' said Pat, but with a hurried farewell the mice left, making for Will's house.

In the morning as Will prepared breakfast, Sam asked him, 'Why can't you remember your spells?'

'I don't know,' answered Will unhappily. 'My mind just flies all over the place in a great big jumble.'

'Surely,' said Sam looking at the books of magic which lined the walls, 'in one of those there must be a spell to help you.'

'Maybe there is,' replied Will doubtfully.

The day passed while Will searched and searched through the books of magic. As evening drew near, at last he found the very spell he needed.

In great excitement he placed the large black pot on the table. With shaking fingers he gathered the ingredients, measuring them carefully, not too little and not too much. Stirring with the long wooden spoon, he repeated over and over the magic words.

The room grew so quiet you could hear a snowflake fall and the darkness outside pressed on the window panes. The mice held their breath, hardly daring to breathe. A little hissing sound came from the pot and a coil of green smoke rose in the air, curling round Will's head. As it disappeared towards the ceiling it was followed by another and then another, until the whole room was filled with swirling, curling smoke.

Will stood with his eyes closed tight. Suddenly he gave a shout of joy.

'I can remember the spells,' he cried. 'Every single one of them.' And so he could, all 365 of them.

After that there was no stopping him and spell after spell tumbled out of his head and into the pot. He stirred and chanted and the magic flew around the room. He did the Christmas spell and the air was filled with the smell of roast turkey. Then the music spell and everything in the room danced, chairs, tables and cupboards. All through the night Will wove his magic, until at last the mice fell down exhausted.

'Let's get out of here,' gasped Henry. 'I can't stand any more of this.'

Even Will had had enough and he tumbled down in a heap snoring loudly.

It was late morning when they all awoke.

'Well, my friends,' said Will, as the mice packed their rucksacks. 'We've had a marvellous time together. I'm sorry you must leave.'

As the mice put on their skis and waved good-bye, Will called after them.

'Did I tell you,' he said, 'that my Granny comes from Cork?'

'Well, that's a turn-up,' said Mr Fielding as the mice skied off. 'His Granny comes from Cork!' and the mice laughed so much they nearly fell.

As they whizzed through the clear frosty air Henry said, 'I would like to have seen Pat again. I really liked him.'

'Well here he is,' said Sam, as skiing along, red scarf flying, black hat aflutter, came the snowman. On his back he carried a large rucksack.

'Bless us and save us,' he shouted, 'I thought I'd missed ye.'

'We were talking about you,' said Sam. 'We wanted to say good-bye.'

'There's no good-bye about it,' said Pat. 'I'm coming with ye.'

'To the far north?' gasped the mice in disbelief.

'All the way,' replied Pat. 'I need a holiday and you need a friend.'

What a happy group skied on, right to the top of the Magic Mountain and down the other side.

11

The North Pole

As the mice and Pat skied down the Magic Mountain, the trees thinned and in the distance they saw a great expanse of ice and snow.

In the shadow of a tall pine a shaggy brown animal was standing. As the mice passed, he crouched low on his short, strong legs. The mice didn't see him, but Pat did.

'A wolverene,' he thought, 'and that means trouble!'

Quickly he slipped in amongst the trees and stood waiting. Down the track padded the wolverene, his eyes fixed on the mice ahead. As he drew level with the snowman, Pat jumped and landed right in his path. The wolverene hit that body of ice with a mighty wallop, which knocked him clean out.

'That's fixed him,' Pat said to himself as he skied after the mice. 'He'll have a right headache when he wakes up.'

As they reached the bottom of the mountainside, a herd of reindeer was grazing, scooping away the snow with their large hooves to eat the grass and moss underneath. Pat was in high spirits as he zig-zagged down the trail. He was going so fast and enjoying himself so much that he skied right in amongst the herd.

'Watch where you're going, you great fat snowman,' shouted the reindeers angrily. 'Have you no manners?'

but Pat only laughed as on he skied.

As the mice approached, the reindeers, with their large branching antlers, seemed enormous. A fine old reindeer raised his head and looked at them.

'Well I never,' he said, 'it's my friends, the three mice. Do you not remember me? I'm Stamper.'

Long ago when the mice met Santa Claus, Stamper was a young reindeer.

'I was Santa's lead reindeer for many years,' he said proudly, 'but now I'm retired.'

When the mice told of their mission to rescue Uncle Bert and Roberta, Stamper grew thoughtful.

'That's a tricky one,' he said. 'You'll need all the help you can get,' and gathering the herd about him they held a meeting.

As the reindeers talked, Pat came rushing back.

'What's keeping ye?' he shouted. 'You're very slow.'

Just then an artic fox, as white as snow, ran by.

'You there,' called Stamper when he saw him. 'Come here.'

As the fox approached, his beautiful tail like a snow drift behind him, he eyed the mice hungrily.

'What do you want?' he asked.

'Do you know the whereabouts of STAR and their leader Evil?' asked Stamper.

'Never heard of them,' answered the fox. 'I don't know who they are.'

'I think you do,' said Stamper. 'I know of your fondness for rats.'

The fox shifted uneasily in the snow.

'They're further north,' he said. 'Just keep travelling,'

and he bolted as fast as he could.

'That doesn't tell us much,' said Stamper, 'but at least we know the direction they took.'

Once more the reindeers talked and when they had finished, Stamper said, 'I will journey with you but first I must return home to prepare.'

So off he went, while Pat and the mice stayed safe with the herd.

The reindeers moved over the snow-covered plains, but as they stopped to feed every minute or two, their progress was slow.

'Aren't they the great dawdlers,' said Pat. 'I hate to travel so slow.'

But back came Stamper at last, pulling a sleigh with jingling bells and a large basket of food on board.

'In you get,' he called. 'Make yourselves comfortable.'

As they climbed in, Henry thought, 'What style!'

Sam thought, 'What comfort!'

Mr Fielding thought, 'What food!'

And Pat thought, 'Let's get moving.'

All that day they travelled. They saw penguins and seals and a walrus or two, but not a sign of STAR.

On the second day the air grew colder still and the landscape became an icy waste, for they had reached the North Pole, the Artic Circle itself.

They passed frozen lakes and rivers with floating ice. The days grew short with more darkness than light.

One day, through the half light, something large loomed ahead.

'What is it?' the mice asked nervously.

'It's T P Bear,' said Stamper.

'What does T P stand for?' asked Mr Fielding.

'P is for Polar,' replied Stamper, 'but I haven't an idea what the letter T means.'

'Probably for Thomas,' said Henry. 'He looks like a Thomas to me.'

'I disagree entirely,' said Mr Fielding. 'Whoever heard of a bear called that?'

'Whoever heard of a mouse called Fielding?' sneered Henry. 'That isn't a mouse name at all.'

'Keep your insults to yourself,' shouted Mr Fielding, and oh dear me, what a row raged.

At last Stamper halted the sleigh.

'Out,' he roared. 'Out or keep quiet,' and not another word was said.

Some time later Henry spoke. 'I would like to apologise,' he said, 'for my rudeness. I think Fielding is a very nice name indeed.'

'I must apologise too,' said Mr Fielding. 'I think that bear was *definitely* called Thomas.'

As they prepared to rest for the night in that barren place, Stamper said, 'There's something wrong. We haven't seen a sign or a trace of rats. We must be on the wrong track.'

Up above in the darkening sky a glaucous gull was flying.

'Hi there,' called Stamper. 'Have you seen any rats?'

'Indeed I have,' replied the gull, 'but you won't find them here. You're too far north.'

'That dratted fox,' said Stamper, 'told us to keep on travelling.'

'And you believed him?' said the gull. 'More fool you. He never tells the truth.'

As Stamper and the gull talked, Pat moved a little apart. He wrapped his scarf round his head until only his coal-black eyes were showing.

'Have you toothache?' asked Sam in concern.

'Indeed and I haven't,' replied Pat. 'It's that bird. I can't stand them.'

'Why ever not?' asked Henry in amazement. 'Birds are nice.'

'It's like this,' replied Pat. 'When I was standing on me mountain top away over in Connemara, a flock of birds came down and began to peck the nose off me. A right job I had to drive them away.'

'Why did they do that?' asked Mr Fielding in surprise.

'Carrot,' said Pat. 'Me poor old nose is a carrot.'

As the mice looked at Pat they noticed for the first

time that his nose was indeed a carrot.

Henry and Mr Fielding's shoulders began to shake.

'Don't laugh,' whispered Sam urgently. 'You'll offend him terribly.'

But it was too late. The laughter exploded, and the one who laughed loudest of all was Pat himself.

As the gull flew off, Stamper turned his sleigh.

'Do you know *now* where to find STAR?' asked the mice.

'I do,' replied Stamper, 'and the news isn't good. We must travel west to Shiverburg Castle, the home of the snowy owls, the voles and the shrews. STAR has driven them out — evicted them, every one — and there they hold Uncle Bert and Roberta captive.'

On they went and Stamper grew quiet and thoughtful.

'Tonight,' he said to himself, 'I must take my sleigh up into the sky. It will be hard for me as I am no longer young, but it's the only way.'

12

Rescue

As the first stars appeared in the sky Stamper stood ready. Inside the sleigh the mice and Pat crouched close together.

'Ready,' called Stamper. His heart beat fast for it was many years since he had taken his sleigh skywards.

Slowly at first, then gathering speed, faster and faster into a full gallop he went.

'I can't do it,' he thought in dejection. 'I've lost the skill,' but he was wrong, for in a smooth flowing movement they took to the air, rising higher and higher.

All through that night they travelled, Stamper tossing his antlered head as he galloped. As the stars faded and the grey dawn approached, he brought his sleigh gently down to earth. As it touched the snow-covered ground, he snorted in the cold morning air.

'I've done it,' he thought triumphantly.

In the distance was a dark forest and as he pulled the sleigh towards the tall trees Stamper became exhausted.

'I must rest,' he said. 'I can't go another step.'

'I'll keep watch,' said Pat. 'Then you can all sleep. If STAR comes I'll deal with them,' and he chuckled as he remembered what he had done to the wolverene.

When Stamper and the mice wakened, Pat was still keeping watch.

'All's quiet,' he said, ' 'tis the emptiest forest I ever saw.'

On they went again through the forest, a dark and gloomy place with deep snow along untravelled paths.

At last they came to a frozen lake, and there beside it were the ruins of Shiverburg Castle. Once a grand family had lived there but they left, driven out by loneliness and cold. The years passed, the floors rotted, the ice and snow made holes in the roof, but the house gave shelter to the animals of the forest and they were happy there.

As the mice looked at that lonely place they felt great fear. From a crumbling tower a flag was flying and on that flag was the dreaded sign ★

'They're here,' whispered Henry and he grew faint.

'We've found them,' croaked Mr Fielding and he grew weak.

'C-c-courage,' stammered Sam and his legs trembled and shook.

The hours passed and not a sound came from the ruin, but as darkness fell something happened at last. From a black, gaping window a light flared, and then another. The great front door creaked open and out poured STAR. Each one held a torch of flame and the dark night blazed with their light. Last of all came Evil and his shadow, large and terrifying, was cast on the castle wall.

'I know you are there,' he shouted. 'You can't hide from me. Soon you will all perish,' and with a terrible laugh which echoed round the forest, he and STAR were gone. The great door closed and the night was black once more.

'We will never see our wives and children again,' wept Henry and his sobs grew louder and louder.

'Control yourself,' said Sam. 'We're not beaten yet.'

As he spoke an owl called softly, as through the trees came a family of snowy owls.

'We will help you,' they said, 'for we have lost our home and suffered much from STAR.'

'We will help too,' more voices called as out from the undergrowth, running and scampering, came weasels, shrews and voles.

All through that dark, terrifying night the animals came, and all had suffered from the wickedness of STAR.

As dawn was breaking the artic foxes arrived. When Stamper saw them he grew angry.

'It was one of you,' he said, 'who sent us the wrong way, right to the North Pole.'

'Not us,' they replied, shaking their heads. 'It must have been the old villain, he never tells the truth.'

Last of all came the old villain himself, as bold as you please.

'Liar!' shouted Stamper when he saw him. 'Vermin! Cheat!'

'Have mercy on me,' whined the fox, 'I meant no harm.'

'No harm,' roared Stamper. 'You sent us to the North Pole and back,' and lunging at the fox he tried to strike him with his antlers.

'If it's a fight ye want,' called Pat, 'save it for STAR. We'll need all our strength for that.'

As night turned to day, once more the castle door opened and Evil strode out. What a sight met his eyes! Everywhere he looked were birds and animals, a great army of them, all ready for battle.

With a strangled cry he ran back inside and banged the door shut.

'What now?' asked Pat. 'When will we strike?'

'Not yet,' replied Stamper. 'We must wait for night.'

As darkness fell the advance guard left. The snowy owls flew like silent shadows towards the castle and slipped in amongst the crumbling walls. The seconds and the minutes ticked by, but no sound came from the ruin.

'What can have happened?' asked the mice. 'The owls should have driven STAR out by now.'

Back came the owls at last.

'They've gone,' they shouted. 'Escaped, every one of them. The place is empty!'

'Uncle Bert and Roberta,' cried the mice. 'Have they gone too?' and before anyone could stop them, they ran to the castle and disappeared inside.

Moonlight filtered through cracks and holes in the castle walls, casting ghostly fingers of light. The air was icy-cold and damp with decay. Through room after room the mice went, searching.

'Uncle Bert,' they called, 'Roberta,' but the walls threw their voices mockingly back.

'We have failed,' said Sam. 'After all this time and travelling so far.'

As the mice retraced their steps with heavy hearts, Mr Fielding paused.

'What's that?' he asked, and they all stood listening.

From far below came a sound.

'Knock, knock, knock,' it went, over and over again.

'Someone's down there,' shouted Sam. 'Come on.'

Stumbling, and nearly falling in the darkness, they came to a flight of stone steps. Down they went, groping in the inky blackness, and every step brought them nearer to that knocking, until they stood with thumping hearts before a heavy iron door.

'Who's there?' called Sam, but no voice answered, only the steady beat of that knocking.

'We must open this door,' said Sam and he began to search for a key.

'It's a trap,' shouted Henry. 'That's STAR inside,' and he turned to run. But before he took more than one step he fell sprawling on the icy floor.

As Sam helped him up, he touched something hard and to his amazement it was a torch. Switching it on, the beam flooded the darkness, and there, in the door, was a rusty key. Sam turned it in the lock and threw the door open. Inside, bound and gagged, were Uncle Bert and Roberta.

With cries of joy the mice rushed forward to tear off the gags and cut the bonds.

'You've come at last,' said Uncle Bert. 'We thought you never would.'

What rejoicing there was then as the mice set them free.

'How did STAR treat you?' asked Sam when the first excitement passed. 'Are you in bad shape?'

'Not in the least,' replied Uncle Bert. 'We were treated quite well.'

'Speak for yourself,' said Roberta. 'I've had an awful time.'

'How's that?' the mice asked anxiously.

'Cooking,' replied Roberta. 'Every day I had to cook every meal.'

'Was that so bad?' asked Mr Fielding, who thought with pleasure of the food.

'It couldn't have been worse,' said Roberta, 'for I simply hate to cook.'

As they talked, the air outside throbbed and roared as a fleet of helicopters passed overhead.

'What's that,' asked the three mice in alarm.

'That's STAR,' replied Roberta. 'Making their escape.'

With the torch to guide them the mice ran back up the stone steps, through dark echoing rooms, and outside. As they stood looking up into the night sky, one helicopter, larger than the rest, hovered overhead, coming lower and lower. The mice cowered in terror as the door opened and Evil appeared. With a shriek which rent the air, he screamed, 'YOU WILL SUFFER FOR THIS ... I WILL TAKE MY REVENGE!'

The door closed, the helicopter rose in the air and was gone.

'What awful deed is he planning?' moaned the mice.

'He's only codding,' said Pat. 'There's nothing to fear.'

As the roar of the helicopters died away, the creatures of the forest let out a great shout of joy. Their enemy had gone. As they returned to their homes in the castle, they sang and danced far into the night. No one sang louder than Uncle Bert, or danced more than Roberta.

When the celebrations ended at last, Uncle Bert told of his capture by STAR.

'I am a rich mouse,' he said, 'with many contacts round the world. On my last business trip to the North Pole I was ambushed by STAR and brought to this place, and here I have been ever since.'

'Was it your money they were after?' asked Henry.

'Indeed it was,' replied Uncle Bert. 'Day after day, week after week, they asked me, "Tell us the secret of your wealth?"'

'And did you tell them?' asked Mr Fielding.

'I told them this story and that,' replied Uncle Bert with a laugh, 'every day a different one, but I never told them the secret.'

82

Then Roberta told how STAR had kidnapped her.

'I left the plane as you slept,' she told the mice. 'As I jogged through the woods STAR appeared, and before I knew what was happening, they had taken me captive.'

'I just knew,' muttered Mr Fielding, 'that no good would come of jogging.'

At last everyone slept, worn out with excitement.

The day was far advanced when they awoke.

'How I long to go home,' said Uncle Bert, as he stood looking at the frozen lake and the dark forest. 'Where are all my children? Are none of them out there searching for us?'

Day after day they waited, but no one came and not a sound was heard in the snow-clad forest. Stamper grew uneasy to return to his herd, and Pat grew impatient to be off too.

'I can't bear this hanging about,' he said as he skied up and down outside the castle.

As the days passed the mice became silent and sad.

When they had almost given up hope, something wonderful happened — they heard a plane.

Over the forest it came, over the frozen lake and the ruined castle, circling lower and lower, until it landed only yards from where they stood. The engine died, the door opened, and out jumped Albert.

'My son,' cried Uncle Bert. 'Rescue at last,' and everyone wept for joy.

13
Revenge

And so Albert told his story.

'We have been searching for many weeks,' he said, 'but there was no sign of you anywhere. Then one day as we flew towards the North Pole, we heard on our radio the voice of Evil as he left Shiverburg Castle. He was in a towering rage, screaming and roaring at his crew.

' "I must have revenge," he shouted. "We will fly to Ireland and invade the town of Wicklow." '

At those dreadful words the three mice cried out in agony.

'Our wives and children,' they wept. 'Who will save them?'

'They are safe,' said Albert. 'We too flew to Wicklow and evacuated them all before STAR arrived.'

'Where are they now?' asked the mice in great distress. 'In what safe place did you put them?'

'They're in the Big House,' answered Albert. 'Guarded by the cats.'

'In *my* house?' said Henry in alarm. 'Henrietta won't like *that*.'

'She's delighted,' answered Albert. 'While you've been away your wives and children have all become great friends.'

'Amazing,' murmured Sam.

'Astonishing,' muttered Mr Fielding.

'Unbelievable,' thought Henry.

But to their surprise, the three mice felt quite pleased.

So the time had come to say good-bye to Stamper and Pat, and the parting was sad.

Big tears ran down Pat's cheeks, turning to icicles as they fell in the snow. Henry, too, sobbed a little, while Sam and Mr Fielding blew their noses hard.

'I'll come and visit ye,' said Pat, 'some day when it snows in Ireland.'

As the plane took off, climbing higher and higher, Pat and Stamper grew smaller and smaller, as they stood below, waving.

And so they set course for Ireland. Over the land and the sea they flew, on and on, hour after hour, until at last the east coast of Ireland drew near. The lights of Wicklow shone like beacons guiding them home.

As Albert made his descent, they saw the harbour and the Murrough and Sam's church ... and then they saw something else. As the moonlight caught the copper dome of the church, a flag was flying, and on that flag was the dreaded sign ★

Evil had taken his revenge!

'They've captured my church,' moaned Sam. 'My home.'

As Henry and Mr Fielding tried to comfort him, Albert brought his plane in to land. As they stepped into the cold night, snowflakes began to fall.

'Would you believe it?' said Uncle Bert. 'The snow has followed us.'

The mice stood on the banks of the Vartry River looking at the church above them. Even as they watched, STAR were working to destroy it, burrowing deep into the earth, undermining the foundations which had stood strong for centuries. Now they saw the full extent of the horror, for slowly but surely, the church was slipping.

Day after day STAR continued their destructive course. The people of the town came and went, shaking their heads, not knowing what to do. Now the snow lay thick on the ground for Ireland was having a long, hard winter.

The weeks passed and one day a ship sailed into the harbour. As it docked, two strange figures disembarked and hurried along the quayside. The people who saw them thought a carnival had come to town.

On the river bank Sam was sitting, bowed down with sorrow. As the strangers approached, he didn't even lift his head.

'Do you not know us?' asked the large white figure. 'We've come to visit you.'

Sam raised his tired eyes, and there stood his friends Pat and Will, all the way from the Far North.

'What has happened to you?' they asked in alarm when they saw how ill Sam looked.

'You may well ask,' he replied, and he told them the whole sorry story.

As they looked at the slipping church, Will said, 'We'll soon fix that. All I have to do is think of a spell.'

'What about your exams?' Sam asked wearily. 'Did you pass them?'

'Every one,' replied Will. 'I'm a fully qualified Wizard now.

'Well done,' said Sam and he even managed a wan smile.

Some days later Evil held a party. Loud music

boomed from the church as STAR enjoyed themselves.

Sam was now so weak with grief he could hardly stand.

'My church,' he moaned, and no one could comfort him.

'What about the spell?' Pat asked Will impatiently. '*Surely* ye've thought of it by now.'

'It takes time,' replied Will. 'I'll think of it yet.'

'That might be too late,' muttered Pat, as he tried once more to comfort Sam.

'Come to the Big House and your family,' said Henry. 'Leave this place to STAR.'

'Never,' said Sam, '*never*', and his thin body shook with his sobbing.

At that moment Will came running. 'I've got it,' he shouted. 'I know the very spell to save the church.'

When STAR heard the noise they stopped work to see what was going on. They were in jubilant mood for Evil had told them that the church would soon fall. They began to jeer at the mice and their friends.

'Pay no attention,' said Will. 'Their days here are numbered.'

The news spread like wildfire that the church would be saved and the streets of Wicklow were jammed as people stood waiting.

When STAR saw this, they worked harder than ever. The great mounds of earth beside the church grew and grew, as they burrowed deeper and deeper. Once Evil appeared on the copper dome shouting at the crowd, but when they threw rotten eggs at him, he hurriedly left.

Will took the magic pot from his suitcase and stood it on the ground. One by one he placed the ingredients inside. At last all seemed ready, but Will stood deep in thought as the crowd grew restless.

'What ails you?' said Pat. 'Can't ye get a move on?'

'I need one thing more,' replied Will, 'and that's music.

'My spell will drive the rats out of the church, but I need music to draw them over the river and down to the sea.'

'I will do that,' said Sam, and from his pocket he took his mouth-organ.

'My dear friend,' said Henry, 'you are too weak and it is too dangerous.'

'There will be little danger,' said Will. 'The rats will be dazed as they leave the church and will follow the music.'

'Sam must not do this alone,' said Mr Fielding. 'We three have suffered much together and will stand united to the end.'

And so the mice took up their position near the edge of the sea. Will began the magic words. The crowd grew silent as a thin puff of smoke drifted skywards. The air grew hot, while a rumble like distant thunder began and died away. Suddenly, with a flash and a roar, a ball of fire shot high into the air. The watching crowd fell back.

'Get the fire brigade,' they shouted. 'He'll burn the church down.'

But the fire-ball died and the air was filled with thick grey smoke, as out of the church, staggering and running, stumbling and falling, came Evil followed by STAR.

'Music,' roared Will, and Sam began to play.

Down the banks poured the rats, into the river they plunged. Swimming strongly, they reached the far side and headed for the sea. As they drew near the three mice, Evil hesitated. He turned his dazed, wicked eyes on them, and Sam faltered.

'Play on,' screamed Will as the music began to fade.

'By the hookey they need help,' cried Pat, and like a streak of lightning he ran down to the water's edge. With two strokes he crossed the river. Just in time he got there, as the rats became a jostling mass around the mice.

'Lay off me buddies,' he shouted and he began to boot the rats into the sea.

At that moment a little wind sprang up, growing stronger by the minute until it roared across the Murrough, and as it went it gathered up the rats in a great black cloud, whirling them out over the Irish sea.

The mice clung to Pat in terror as they watched it go, for they had nearly gone with it.

On the coast of Wales, people stared as a huge black cloud appeared, coming nearer and nearer. When it reached land it hovered, before raining down hundreds of large ugly rats.

'A plague of rats,' cried everyone as they ran into their houses and slammed the doors shut.

In the town of Wicklow a shout of triumph rose

from all who saw that cloud of darkness disappear.

'That's got rid of them,' said Will in delight. 'Now we'll save the church.'

'I must see the damage,' said Sam, and before anyone could stop him he rushed in amongst the slipping foundations, and through the dark tunnels where STAR had dug deep into the earth. The sound of running water filled the air, for an underground stream had been uncovered.

'There is not a minute to lose,' he thought as he staggered out again.

'The church is about to fall,' he screamed, and then he fainted.

When Sam came to, Will was preparing another spell.

'Be quick,' he called as everyone ran here and there, gathering ingredients. But at last all was ready.

As Will began the magic words, the crowd held their breath and even the birds stopped singing.

'What if it doesn't work?' whispered Henry as he looked at Sam lying pale and faint on the ground.

But it did work.

Once more the church stood straight and tall, with its copper dome shining. What rejoicing there was then with the church bells ringing, the clock striking, the organ playing, and Sam fully recovered.

Some days later Pat and Will stood on the quayside, ready to board their ship to the far north.

'Will you not stay?' asked Sam.

'You could visit your granny in Cork,' said Mr Fielding to Will.

'And your friends in Connemara,' said Henry to Pat. But they shook their heads.

'It's time to leave,' said Will. 'Our journey will be long.'

'If I stay I'll melt,' said Pat looking at the thawing snow and the blue sky.

As the ship sailed out of the harbour, it hooted twice. On the deck, the white figure of Pat and the strange figure of Will stood waving. The mice watched until the ship grew faint, and the curling wake disappeared from sight. Then they turned sadly away.

But there were more good-byes to be said, for Uncle Bert was leaving, going home, at last, to Aunt Bertha.

As Roberta and Albert checked their plane and tuned the engine, the mice stood watching.

'Will you get married soon?' Sam asked Roberta. 'I hear you have a French boy-friend.'

'You mean Pierre?' replied Roberta. 'Pierre de Flirt. Oh no! I won't marry him. I'm off to South America to travel the Amazon.'

As the plane taxied to the end of the field, the mice and their families waved a last farewell.

14
Happy Ever After

Sam the church-mouse closed the door of his sound-proof study, pocketed his book of *Memoirs*, Vol 3, and strode outside.

Mr Fielding took a health-food pie from his microwave oven, did a few turns on his exercise-bike and ran out into the sunshine.

Henry the house-mouse pulled on his red boots and yellow mac, revved up his motor-bike and roared down the driveway, terrifying the cats.

Under the church clock the three mice met and began to walk down the hill towards the river.

'I must say,' said Mr Fielding, 'that Uncle Bert's presents have been most useful . . . a sound-proof study, a microwave oven, an exercise-bike and a motor-cycle. What else could you want?'

'We couldn't agree more,' said Henry and Sam, as on down Church Hill they ambled.

Some day, if you look carefully and if you are lucky, you might see Henry and Sam and Mr Fielding, Special Agents, walking by the river. For the three mice, their wives and children, really did live happily ever after.

THE END!

VERA PETTIGREW was born and educated in Northern Ireland but came south when she married Stanley Pettigrew, who was until recently Rector of Wicklow town. She spent many years of her life living in remote areas of County Wicklow — hence her fondness for mice, the patter of whose tiny feet kept her and her family company on dark winter nights.

Now living in a house that overlooks the Murrough near Wicklow town, she is actively involved in the Society for the Prevention of Cruelty to Animals, Guide Dogs for the Blind, and the Wicklow Adult Literacy Scheme.

This is her third book. The other two are:

The Adventures of Henry & Sam & Mr Fielding
Introducing the three mice, who all longed to have a great Adventure, and what befell them in their search for the Land of Milk and Honey.
Illustrated by Al O'Donnell. Paperback £2.50

Fionuala the Glendalough Goat
Fionuala, a goat of inquiring mind, is determined to find her ancestors, the Cool-Boys of Glendalough. After very many adventures she gets to Glendalough ... and what a surprise she finds there.
Illustrated by Terry Myler. Paperback £3.96